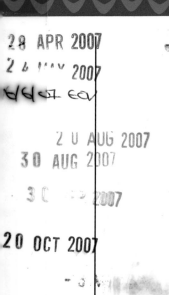

Copyright © Spellbound Entertainment Limited and Famous Flying Films Limited 2004
Published by Ladybird Books Ltd
A Penguin Company
80 Strand, London WC2R 0RL
Penguin Books Australia Ltd., Camberwell, Victoria, Australia
Penguin Books (NZ) Lt.l., Private Bag 102902, NSMC, Auckland, New Zealand

www.ladybird.co.uk

13 5 7 9 10 8 6 4 2

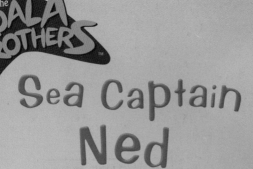

The Koala Brothers

Sea Captain Ned

Ladybird

One day, Ned, the little wombat, decided to go for a walk.

It was lovely walking weather for wombats. The sun was high in the sky and blazing down over the outback. Ned was pottering along when he came upon something unusual. Or rather, he *tripped* over it.

Someone had left a wooden peg in the ground. Ned picked it up. It was attached to a rope that twisted and coiled out of sight. But where did it lead to?

Ned followed the rope to see if he could find out.

Ned couldn't believe his eyes. At the end of the rope there was a boat!

Ned was very excited. He couldn't wait to show the Koala Brothers.

Frank and Buster were at their homestead, cleaning the plane.

"Hello, Frank! Hello, Buster!" Ned called. "Look what I've found! It's very nice, don't you think?"

"Er . . . yes, Ned," Frank and Buster said, uncertainly. The boat didn't look like it could ever float.

Ned saluted them both. "I've decided to become a sea captain!" he said.

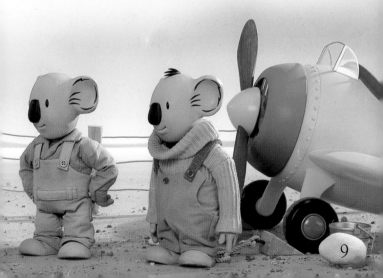

9

"This is going to be my ship,"
Ned went on. "It'll need a bit
of work, of course. But there's
something I have to do first!"

Ned nipped off, and returned . . .

. . . wearing a sailor's hat.

"You look just like a real sea captain!" smiled Frank. "I'm a bit worried about your ship though. It might be too broken to fix!"

There was a big hole in the bottom, no sail, no rudder and no ship's wheel. Really, it was more of a shipwreck than a ship.

Ned sighed, and looked very sad.

Frank and Buster hated to see Ned upset so they offered to help him fix his boat. "We're the Koala Brothers – we're here to help!" they told him.

They found their tools and set to work on Ned's battered old boat. They hammered and sawed and painted and polished. They rigged up a rudder and sorted out a sail and whipped up a ship's wheel – and they saluted Captain Ned.

They saluted Captain Ned *a lot.*

Soon, the boat was looking much better. Ned could barely contain his excitement.

Just then, Mitzi turned up. "You
made a ship!" she shouted, amazed.
"Where are you going to sail it?
You'll need lots of water."

"Water?" Ned said in a small voice.

"You must have thought of water!"
cried Mitzi. "How can you sail a
boat without water?"

Ned began to walk away sadly.

Where could they find enough
water out here in the outback?

Suddenly, Buster had a brainwave.
"Frank . . ." he began.

"The waterhole!" Frank cried.
He'd had the same great idea!

"That's it!" Ned yelled, excited
all over again. "We'll drag the
ship down to the waterhole!"

But it wasn't so easy. Though
they huffed and puffed and
heaved and shoved for ages,
they just couldn't shift it.

"The ship's too heavy," wailed Ned.

"We'll never push it to the water-hole!" The Koala Brothers sighed.

"Maybe you should just put it on wheels," suggested Mitzi.

And that's just what they did.

Soon, with Captain Ned proudly at the helm, the ship set sail for its first fantastic journey.

Alice was enjoying some tea at the waterhole with Archie. "It's so quiet here," she sighed, happily. "Just us and the sound of crickets."

"And the odd sailing ship," Archie added, his eyes widening.

The *very* odd sailing ship, thought Alice. It wasn't crickets she'd heard, but the sound of squeaky wheels as Ned's splendid ship approached the waterhole.

"Hi, Alice. Hi, Archie!" called
Frank. "We've built a ship for Ned!
We were wondering if we could
sail it in the waterhole?"

"Go ahead!" cried Alice and Archie.

The big moment had arrived.
Everyone gathered around. Ned
was finally going to sail his ship!

With a big heave, they launched the ship with a splendid splash.

There was a grinding, groaning, grating sound, and the ship stopped. 'I'm stuck!' yelled Ned.

"It's the water," Frank realised, "it's not deep enough!"

"This is no good," Ned sulked.
"I can't be a real sea captain in a
waterhole!" He clambered out of
the ship and stalked off – splosh,
splash, splish – out of the waterhole
and off into the distance.

"I think he's upset," Frank said to
Mitzi. They turned to go after him.

"But you can't just leave the ship
here," Alice told them, a little put
out. "It's in the way!"

So, while everyone else helped pull Ned's ship out of the water, Buster went to talk to Ned. He found him slumped by a rock, his special hat lying in the dust.

"It's not fair," grumbled Ned. "I just wanted to be a real captain."

Buster thought hard. "Maybe you can still be a sea captain, if you really want to."

Ned didn't look convinced. "How?"

Buster picked up the captain's hat
and plonked it back on Ned's head.
"Frank will think of something!"
he promised.

And Buster was right. While the others rested after pulling the ship out of the waterhole, Frank was thinking of an idea.

First, he checked the wheels. Then he raised the sail. It rippled as it caught the warm breeze.

Buster came bounding up. "Frank, we're going to have to help Ned."

"I think," said Frank, quietly, "with just a bit more breeze . . ."

Suddenly, to everyone's amazement, the sail caught enough wind to start pulling the ship along on its creaky old wheels.

"Frank!" gasped Buster, hopping up and down with excitement. "You've done it! The ship – it's sailing!"

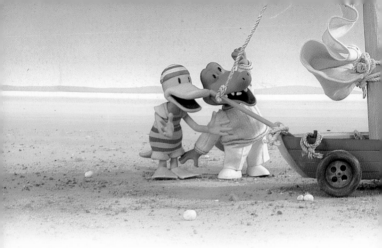

Buster dashed off to fetch Ned and tell him the good news – he could be a sea captain after all!

As Ned took his place at the wheel of the ship, everyone gathered round to wish him well. And this time, the launch was a big success.

"Look at Ned!" said Buster, happily, as the ship creaked noisily away.

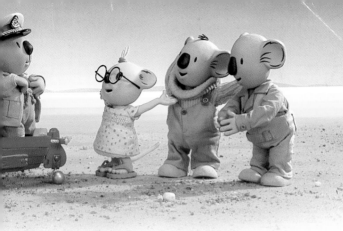

"You mean *Captain* Ned!" Frank smiled.

So, with the Koala Brothers' help, Ned really did get to sail his ship – even without the sea! And Captain Ned was the proudest sea captain ever to sail the outback.

The General Store

Alice's House

Post Office

The Post